A note from the author . . .

What would you think if you were given a plant for your birthday? I bet you wouldn't be very excited and would much rather have unwrapped an X-Box.

But what if it's no ordinary plant. First it eats flies, and then burgers start disappearing from the barbecue. The more it eats, the more the plant grows, and grows. Until it's hungry for something much bigger than burgers . . .

I hope you enjoy my scary story, and think twice before going near your house plants again!

Dina Anastasio

EEK!

STORIES TO MAKE YOU SHRIEK!

Fly Trap

Dina Anastasio

Illustrated by Simon Cooper

MACMILLAN CHILDREN'S BOOKS

Text first published 1996 by Putnam & Grosset Group, USA
Text reprinted by permission of Penguin Putnam Books for Young Readers,
a division of Penguin Putnam Inc

This edition published 1999 by Macmillan Children's Books
a division of Pan Macmillan Limited
20 New Wharf Road, London N1 9RR
Basingstoke and Oxford
www.panmacmillan.com

In association with Virgin Trains

ISBN 0 330 37128 2

5 7 9 8 6

A CIP catalogue record for this book is available from the British Library.

Printed and bound in Great Britain by Mackays of Chatham plc, Kent

It all started on my birthday.

Every year I have a party.

Every year my friends come.

Buddy comes too.

Buddy lives next door.

Buddy is a pain.

But Mum makes me ask him.

This year, Aunt Sarah was there.
Aunt Sarah goes all over the world.
And she always gives the best
birthday presents.

One year she gave me a puppet
from China.

Last year I got drums from Africa.

This year she gave me a plant.

A plant?

"This is not just any plant," Aunt
Sarah said. "This is a fly trap."

"Oh," I said.

"It eats bugs," she said.

"OH!" I said.

"That's the dumbest present I've ever seen," Buddy said.

Like I said, Buddy is a pain.

Just then a little fly buzzed by.

"Watch," my aunt said.

We all watched.

BUZZ, BUZZ, BUZZ.

The little fly buzzed over to the plant.

The plant opened its little jaws.

BUZZ!

The fly flew in.

SNAP!

The jaws slammed shut.

No more fly!

9

"Wow!" everybody said – everybody but Buddy.

"It's still a dumb present," Buddy said.

Aunt Sarah smiled.

"Your plant is easy to take care of," she told me. "Just put it outside. It feeds itself.

But there is one rule you must never break. Never, ever feed meat to the plant.

If you do . . ."

HONK, HONK.

A car horn was honking.

"Oh, my," said Aunt Sarah. "That is my ride.

I am flying to Bora Bora tonight."

13

And Aunt Sarah was gone.

Buddy came over the next day.

I was outside with my plant.

Buddy was eating a hot dog.

And he was carrying a snake.

A big snake.

It even had a lead.

"Check it out," Buddy said. "This is a real present! My dad gave it to me. And it's not even my birthday."

Boy, Buddy is a pain!

Buddy walked over to the plant.

He watched it eat a big, black fly.

"Flies! Aren't you sick of eating
flies?" Buddy said to the plant.
"Here! Have a little hot dog."

19

Buddy tossed some hot dog to the plant.

"No!" I yelled.

But I was too late.

SNAP!

No more hot dog!

My aunt had said, "Never, ever feed meat to the plant. If you do . . ."

If you do . . . what?

Aunt Sarah never said.

Well, now I would find out.

That night, we had a barbecue.

My dad was cooking burgers.

They were thick and round.

Yum!

I looked over at my plant.

Its little jaws opened and closed.

Was the plant hungry too?

Dad and I went in to get plates.
We came back a minute later.

Something was wrong.

"That's funny," my dad said. "I
know I put six burgers on the grill.
And now there are five."

I did not say anything.

I looked at the plant.

Funny. It did not look hungry
now.

The next morning, I put birdseed
in the bird feeder. It is my job. There
are always lots of birds.

But not that day. There were no
birds at all.

Just a lot of feathers.

I bent down to pick one up.

SNAP!

OW!

What was that? I turned around.

The plant bit me!

I thought about the plant all day at school.

Aunt Sarah was right. It was not just any plant.

And it was starting to scare me.

My mum was in the yard when I got home. She pointed to the plant.

"That thing looks more like a bear trap than a fly trap," she said.

She was right.

The plant was bigger.

Something was wrong.

"Keep away from that plant,

Mum," I said.

Then I ran inside. I called Aunt
Sarah.

"I'm in Bora Bora. Leave a
message. I will call back," her
machine said.

"Hey, Aunt Sarah," I said. "Phone
me! Please! What happens if you feed
meat to the fly trap? I need to know!"

I sat by the phone.

I waited and waited. A little later, the doorbell rang.

DING-DONG.

It was Buddy. Boy, he was mad!

"Give me back my snake!" he shouted. "I saw it go under your fence!

And I want it back!"

I did not want to go outside.

But I helped Buddy look for his snake.

I had a funny feeling that I knew where it was.

We looked and looked.

No snake.

Then we saw the lead.

It was on the ground.

It was right next to the plant.

"What happened to your plant?
It's so big!" said Buddy.

I did not answer.

RING, RING.

The phone was ringing.

I ran to get it.

Yes!

It was Aunt Sarah.

"I got your message, dear," she said. "I have to make this quick. The answer is: if you feed meat to the fly trap, it will want more . . .

and more . . .

and more."

Yes!

It was true!

It all came together.

The burger.

The birds.

Buddy's snake.

All meat!

All gone!

Ever since Buddy fed the plant his hot dog. It had even tried to bite me!

What would the hungry plant want next?

I looked out of the window. Buddy
was next to the plant.

The plant's jaws were opening.

BUDDY!

"I've got to go!" I told Aunt Sarah.

I ran outside.

"Buddy! Get away from the plant!" I yelled.

Of course he did not listen.

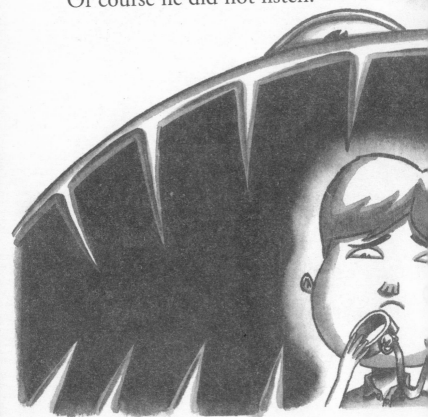

I had no time to lose . . .

I grabbed my mother's clippers.

"Out of my way, Buddy!" I yelled.

I ran over to the plant.

SNIP!

"Hey!" Buddy cried. "Watch it!
You almost got me!"

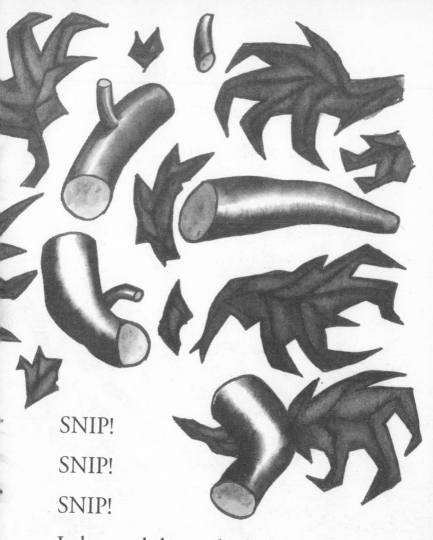

SNIP!

SNIP!

SNIP!

I chopped down the hungry plant.

Soon it was just a big stick.

I was still holding the clippers.

Buddy stared at me. He backed away.

"You must be crazy," he said.

"Crazy, crazy, crazy! You just killed your new plant.

And you almost clipped me!"

Was I crazy?

Or had I just saved Buddy's life?

Who knows?

But I do know this:

Buddy never bugs me any more!

SUSAN PRICE

Olly Spellmaker
and the
Hairy Horror

**Hairy Bill, the helpful bogle,
seemed harmless. At first . . .**

Since he arrived at Alex Matheson's home, Hairy Bill hasn't stopped polishing and vacuuming. Which means no more chores! But dusting is only the beginning for Hairy Bill – he soon has scary plans to take over the whole house.

When the Mathesons call for help, motorbike-riding witch Olly Spellmaker comes to the rescue. With her new bogle-busting assistant, Alex, Olly can handle anything. But she's never had to fight a Hairy Horror!

VIVIAN FRENCH

WICKED CHICKENS

Charlie's dad has won at the bingo and now the family can move to his dream home – one with roses round the door and hens scratching in the yard – whether they like it or not.

They don't! Dad's dream turns out to be a nightmare and as for the fowl, they're foul. Those birds are scary. Charlie's not chicken but their glittering eyes are always watching.

Nobody believes Charlie – until the morning Mum pulls back the curtains and gets a terrible fright.

Dad's dreams have come home to roost . . . and what has happened to those chickens?

TERENCE BLACKER

>YOU HAVE GHOST MAIL<

Help me and I shall help you . . .

Matthew has always wanted a new computer. But now that he has been given one for his birthday, something strange and frightening is happening. It seems that someone is trying to contact him from cyberspace – someone who died fifty years ago.

An email from the spirit zone? At first Matthew doesn't believe it. But soon it is more than a computer that is being possessed by the ghostly power of a visitor from beyond the grave.